Dark Passenger

First Love Cuts The Deepest
Volume 1

MATTHEW TAYVONNE

BALBOA.
PRESS
A DIVISION OF HAY HOUSE

Balboa Press books may be ordered through booksellers or by contacting:

Balboa Press
A Division of Hay House
1663 Liberty Drive
Bloomington, IN 47403
www.balboapress.com
1 (877) 407-4847

Because of the dynamic nature of the Internet, any web addresses or
links contained in this book may have changed since publication and
may no longer be valid. The views expressed in this work are solely those
of the author and do not necessarily reflect the views of the publisher,
and the publisher hereby disclaims any responsibility for them.

The author of this book does not dispense medical advice or prescribe the use
of any technique as a form of treatment for physical, emotional, or medical
problems without the advice of a physician, either directly or indirectly. The
intent of the author is only to offer information of a general nature to help
you in your quest for emotional and spiritual well-being. In the event you use
any of the information in this book for yourself, which is your constitutional
right, the author and the publisher assume no responsibility for your actions.

Any people depicted in stock imagery provided by Thinkstock are
models, and such images are being used for illustrative purposes only.
Certain stock imagery © Thinkstock.

Print information available on the last page.

ISBN: 978-1-5043-4177-6 (sc)
ISBN: 978-1-5043-4178-3 (e)

Balboa Press rev. date: 12/28/2015

Acknowledgment & Dedications

This book is dedicated to all of its readers. Life is truly what you make it and we only get one, so I say Live it to the fullest. Go after your dreams and never take no, or you can't for an answer. You can do anything you want with hard work and dedication. Whatever you do, make sure it comes from a place of peace and love. Enjoy reading the first volume of this three part series.

Without the Lord our savior, I would not be here today and I am forever grateful for his continued blessings upon my life. My family is everything to me and through my rights and wrongs they stand beside me. Thank you to my beautiful mother (Crystal), grandmother (Queen), and my family. I love you guys with all my heart. My family is my world.

To learn a little More About Me, you can follow me on all my Social Media. I would love to hear from you.

FaceBook: Matthew Tayvonne
IG & Twitter: MatthewTayvonne
Website: www.TheUtopiaSuite.com

Thank you to everyone who has supported me and believed in my dream. I truly appreciate all of your feedback and support since the beginning of my writing.

Photography by: Blair Devereaux for Pheauxtography", Nathan Percy of NP Photography. Model/Actor: Andrew Ghent, Special Thanks to David Snyder & DeAngelo Green, David A Rice, Danny Jackson, J'Lamar Nichols, lynnell Scott, Deandre Burgan, Sherry Tyree, Torrance Nowden, Courtney Robinson, Vicky Boyd, Shakia Cook, Shira Solomon, Michael Morgan, Alonzo Clark, Ebonie Lee, Al K Edwards, Waki Henderson, Kelli Jacobs, Latisha Sloan, Kivan Pennington, La'Daunte Ecckles-Clay, Crystal Mason, Savannah Harris, Brandon Lee, Tony Rutherford, Nicole Simmons, Autumn Montgomery, Michelle Rasoletti, Mike Brown,, Darius Brown, Timothy Patrick, Asante Moore, Jae Dumas, Nelson Irabor.

Acclaim For Matthew Tayvonne Dark Passanger

First Love Cuts The Deepest

February of 2012 we were auditioning models for THE F.A.B. EVENT FASHION AGAINST BULLYING first show here in Atlanta. During the audition process a young man walked through the door and introduced himself to me and the other founders and people involved as MATTHEW TAYVONNE…. with one shake of the hand I knew there was more to Matthew than meets the eye.

3 years and many stories later, what I saw in Matthew that day is now coming to fruition. Matthew or son, as I call him, is a gifted story teller. Matthew's stories are based on a gift to tell the truth of A JOURNEY. A truth that comes from allowing himself to live out loud and be proud of who

he is and the world he walks in. There is a Grace Gift to how Matthew puts feelings to words and draws you into feel as if you are reading and watching a movie at the same time. Only a few writers have that gift.

In this story you will be taken on a journey that I believe is personal, heartfelt, mysterious, intense, passionate. Filled with desire and danger. A search for Unconditional Love, Love of Self, Forgiveness, Anger, Pain. Most of all you will finish this book knowing and understanding each character is someone we know and maybe someone who needs our love.

Matthew you are truly like a son to me and I am so proud to see you finish your first of many stories. I have had the pleasure to style you for photo shoots and fashion shows and the esteemed pleasure of reading your stories and being interviewed by you. Remember continue to stay open to God's guidance and open to Love.

David Anthony Rice Owner/Lead Stylist Nuvizions INTL

Chapter One

"Alone"

I'm Damien Hill, a 25 year old college student. I pretty much try to maintain control of every aspect of my life. Every single solitary detail. I can't be left unsure of what's going on. I did that before and it left me confused, scared, and alone. I wasted my time writing love songs, thinking that life was one big fairy tale, hoping to find prince charming.

I thought I had met him in Florida attending college, but he didn't love me. He couldn't have loved me. If he had, he wouldn't have hurt me, and left me feeling like shit! I could give you the whole background story about how he screwed me over, cheated, and everything else under the sun, but I won't. I'm not one of the lucky ones. I don't like to think about it. I don't like to focus on the past but what if the past is my present, something I'm reminded of everyday.

We all are dealt a hand from God right? And this is the hand he dealt me, so what do I do? I deal with it as best as I can, even though my faith is broken and shattered into a million pieces. I will never be the same. I miss who I used to be. Carefree and vibrant, fun and loving. A young man with a sincere heart full of pure gold. Nowadays, I am all about school, work, and no room for games. "Fuck these niggas", that's my motto now. I'm all about the paper now! I'm only concerned with me, myself and I.

Oct 1st

The chills and cold sweat jolt me awake, it's been happening every night, right at 12am. I look over on the left side of the bed expecting to see him, to smell his scent, to wait for him to say, "Bae lay back down", but not anymore, not this time. I can still hear his voice in my head as if he were beside me. I couldn't go back to sleep that night. I roll over again and it's already nine in the morning and it was time for class.

Of course I slow dragged while getting myself together and I was extremely late to my lecture class about societal views on blah blah and more blah. Gay rights, White Supremacy, you name it. Long story short, I feel our society still has a lot of learning and growing to do and this class is a bunch of bullshit.

I walked into lecture class trying to remain incognito but of course that did not happen.

"Mr. Hill, I'm glad you decided to join us, your partner is sitting right next to you, he will fill you in on the group assignment," said Professor Maxwell.

I look to my right and there he was. The most conceited gay boy in the whole entire college. It was mother-fucking Christopher Brown. His big know it all attitude always irritated the hell out of me. Here he goes, smiling and winking at me. I straight faced his ass and looked down at my notes. This is going to be a long semester.

After class I proceeded to walk out. I had nothing to say to Christopher, I just wanted to get to my next course on time.

"Slow down shawty, don't you want me to fill you in on our project," said Christopher.

"Not really," I replied.

"Oh so it's true what they say, you really are a bitch," Christopher uttered.

I was definitely not expecting him to say that. It made me giggle.

"Listen Christopher, Chris baby, Chrissy girl, meet me at Starbucks on campus at 5pm and we can go over everything."

"Fine and I'm not a girl," Christopher proclaimed as he walked off.

It was 5:30pm and Christopher was late. It had been a long day of classes and I wanted to head back to my apartment and rest. Christopher was 6'2" dark chocolate, with a bomb ass body, tattoos with dark brown eyes and silky jet black hair shaped into a Mohawk. He was extremely attractive, but none of those things mattered to me anymore. I'm over that he look good and he has a nice body phase. I'm only interested in my studies, point blank period. Christopher's looks will get him nowhere with me. Plus I heard rumors of his running through boys at the College.

Here comes his dumb ass now I thought to myself.

"Sorry I'm late, I picked us up some snacks, Twizzlers, Snickers, Reese cups. It's a peace treaty for earlier, I didn't mean the whole bitch comment," said Christopher.

I grabbed the Twizzlers. "It's all good, plus Twizzlers are my favorite."

We started to go over the project and to my surprise he's a very smart guy. We stayed there for about 2 hours discussing different ideas and our dislike of Professor Maxwell. Time just seemed to breeze by. Shockingly, I actually enjoyed his conversation.

"Next week your spot Saturday night, just because I'm going to be extremely busy and Saturday night is when I am free," said Christopher.

"I guess that'll be fine." I replied hesitantly

"Cool," Christopher said, with a warm friendly smile.

I didn't know why he wanted to meet at my apartment but whatever. The sooner we get this done, the sooner he will be out of my hair.

Chapter Two

"Christopher Brown's Truth"

Saturday came around and Christopher showed up at my apartment with groceries. He had on black jogging pants, I couldn't help but to look down and sure enough my eyes landed right on his dick print. Bulging out, as if it were looking back at me. I started smiling, hoping he didn't catch me. I couldn't help but to look at his bulge. I quickly snapped out of it before my mind started wondering.

"Someone's happy to see me" said Christopher with a big smile on his face.

He had on a tight white shirt, showcasing his chocolate arms. All I saw was muscles. Again, I had to snap myself out of daydreaming about his large arms around me.

I was so baffled as to why he had groceries in his hands.

"What's all this"? I asked while pointing at the groceries

"We can make spaghetti together and I brought you some Twizzlers," Christopher said with a big smile on his face.

"Well, I guess that's fine" I said smiling back. I led Christopher to the kitchen and he began to cook. I assisted him, taking instructions and of course giving my opinions. I haven't cooked with anyone since my ex, so this felt a little weird and I was enjoying this moment.

Christopher turned out to be an exceptional cook. I love a man that knows his way around the kitchen. Dinner was amazing, we laughed and enjoyed each other's conversation all night long. The wine he brought added a finishing touch, something I didn't expect from him. We actually accomplished a lot, and come to find out we had more in common than I assumed.

After dinner, Christopher went to the bathroom, in search of medicine to feed his wine induced headache.

"My head hurts. Do you have any medicine?"

I quickly rushed him out the bathroom before he touched the medicine cabinet.

"I'm all out."

I lead him to the couch to finish up our work. In the midst of our silence, Christopher leaned over and kissed me. His perfect soft brown lips engulfed mine. It was the best kiss I've had in a while. Matter of fact he was the first kiss I've had all year. Before letting myself slip, I pulled away. I couldn't believe he did that. I laughed uncomfortably.

"I'm sorry," said Christopher.

I shook my head and smiled.

"I should be getting back home to check on my mother. She's sick, she has cancer."

My eyes widen with disbelief. Cancer! I couldn't even imagine what he could be going through.

"Oh wow, she will get through this, we all have things we have to deal with" I said.

"I never share that with anybody, but I feel so comfortable with you. Talking to you seems to put me at ease. I put on this big facade and walk through campus like I don't have not one care in the world, but Damien I do care and I believe God will get her through this. For a while I was just sleeping with different dudes to help mask the pain. That didn't help one bit, just caused more drama. I'm older and more mature now. I trust in the Lord every day and I know he will make a way. Well let me head on out of here and thanks for listening" Christopher replied as he walked out the door. I stopped him and gave him a long hug.

"Thank you for sharing that with me" I said.

The most charming smile flashed across his face as he disappeared into the night. Was he different? Everything that I'd previously thought about Christopher, was it a lie? Momma always said "never judge a book by its cover", he actually had a heart. The rest of the night, Christopher stayed on my mind. I thought about what a nice person he was and how he must have a lot to deal with, concerning the care of his mother.

Before I went to sleep, I said a prayer for Christopher and his mom. Prayer was something I didn't do often anymore, but it felt just right for some reason. I wanted to help him, be there for him but I wasn't ready for all that so I prayed on it, I prayed for him. Apart of me wondered, was God still listening to my prayers because I haven't prayed in so long.

Chapter Three

"My Truth"

Slowly but surely Christopher started making his way not only into my life but into my heart. He started to come over more and more, we started going out to eat, he even got me back in church.

Because of Christopher I was rebuilding my relationship with the Lord. Christopher's enthusiasm for church reminded me of how I used to be, and in his eyes there was only one answer to a problem, prayer. He made my heart feel things I vowed never to feel again. This could be the real Damien around Christopher, this could be the relationship I've always dreamed of. I tried to keep him in the "friend zone" but we both knew what we felt was far beyond friendship. I was letting myself slip and he found the key to my heart. I just pray if I slip and fall he's there to catch me.

Christopher's mother was in the hospital, she was getting worse and had been there for a few weeks so I really hadn't got the chance to talk to Christopher as much, and I completely understood. It as a cold winter night and all I could think about was Christopher. I wondered if he was okay and if his mother was making progress in her fight for life. I laid in bed and listened as the rain hit the roof of my apartment. The rain always had a calming effect on me, but when the thunder begins to roll, I tuck my tail like a puppy and hide underneath the covers.

I decided to read the bible but I couldn't decide on what to read. I thought about Psalms since it's full of prayers. The same prayers I would read every morning to start my day, my favorite Psalms passage is Psalms 91st. A passage of healing and protection. I had just grabbed the bible and suddenly there was a knock at the door. At this time of night no one should be at my door. The thunder clashed loudly and the flashes from the lightening kept me on edge. I peeked through the peep hole and it was Christopher. It was as if everything I read in "The Secret" was true, the law of attraction brought him to my door step. I frantically opened the door, trying to get him out of the rain but it was too late he was soaked. Once he entered the door he sat on the couch and broke down crying.

"I can't deal with this shit anymore, Damien." Christopher sobbed.

I held him close to my heart. I could feel his warm tear drops falling on my chest. I cradled him tight. I know he has been under so much pressure with college courses, and his mother's health.

"Don't cry, you need to get out of these clothes, you're so wet, and you're going to get sick." I replied.

Candles filled the darkness all around my house. My grandma always said "lights off when it's lightening."

I knew he was probably cold, so I went and found him an oversized shirt and some basketball shorts. For some strange reason he followed me in the bedroom, I turned around and he started to take off his shirt. I sat on the bed and watched him as his wet muscles glistened in the candle light. He then took off his pants and following that his briefs. I had to turn the other way because being that close to him literally naked made my dick throb.

"You can look, it's all yours if you want it to be." Christopher said.

I slowly closed my thighs, trying to mask my erection. I handed him the basketball shorts, to put on.

"It's something I need to tell you." I blurted out.

I felt my heart racing, even breathing had become a task. I looked into his eyes, I opened my mouth and nothing came out!

I looked away and the tears began to roll, I shook my head. I thought to myself, "I am in control of this situation. I don't care what he thinks."

I looked him back in his eyes.

"Christopher I'm H..."

Christopher quickly cut me off and finished my sentence "I.V. Positive, I know."

I was so shocked, mouth wide open and couldn't utter a word.

"I knew months ago, I went through your medicine cabinet, I know why you wouldn't just let yourself go around me. It is okay, I love you, and I respect you. You are no different from me. I will never look at you differently because you're not. HIV is not what it was before, I've done my research, trust me. I've just been waiting for you to tell me, so don't cry". Christopher said.

I was in disbelief, it felt like a burden was lifted off of my shoulders and from my heart! For the first time I felt like myself, I felt normal. He began to kiss me on my neck.

"Damien I love you, let me have your heart," Christopher whispered.

I let him take my shirt off, He laid me on my back and started kissing me all over. "You're beautiful" Christopher said.

I pulled him close and whispered in his ear, "I'm all yours, and I'll let you lead the way."

He looked me in my eyes and slid my briefs off. I watched him as he pulled out the condom.

He smiled at me and said "You're in good hands."

He began to ease his manhood in me, I felt the initial pain but I wanted it. I wanted him to make me hurt so damn good. I'm finally letting go and feeling love. I pulled him close and made him go deeper, his dick was so big, so thick and so black!

He moaned out "Damn Damien, Damn Baby, I been waiting for this ass, this moment."

He flipped me over, holding me close with one arm as I was on top riding him fitting his dick like a glove. His chocolate skin felt so smooth against mine. This was it, this was the drive, this was more than just fucking, this was a connection, and this was spiritual. This was love.

Finally feeling loved and I was the passenger. I rode him with one hand on his firm chest and the other on the head board. My red sheets covered different parts of our bodies exposing his chocolate skin and my warm brown skin.

He was so deep inside. I never knew how good this would feel. He was inside of me, making me experience pleasure and pain at the same time. I looked up at the ceiling and all I saw was white and red. It seemed as if the flames from the candles were touching the ceiling forming a circle around us. I was high off of his chocolate dick and I didn't want him to take it out.

"Ride dis dick Baby" Christopher said. I rode harder and looked in his eyes as I bounced up and down. Somehow we ended up on the floor, with me on my back. The coldness of the wooden floor pierced my skin. He was breaking me all the way in, and with every stroke I became more and more wet.

Christopher started to kiss me passionately. He began to shake inside of me and I knew he was coming to a climax. He yelled out loudly as he filled me with his passion and to my surprise, he crawled down and began sucking my dick until I bust all over his chest.

"I love you Damien Hill," Christopher whispered.

"I love you too," I replied.

Chapter Four

"My Past Returns"

We laid there for a moment both high off of making love. He offered me some Waffle House and I agreed. We both started laughing as he pulled the cum filled condom off. He quickly hopped up and grabbed my hand. He led me to the shower and we washed each other off. Christopher's chiseled and toned body looked even more amazing in the shower.

"You wanna go again" said Christopher with a devilish smirk on his face.

I shook my head and we both started laughing but I knew he was serious and he wanted some more of this ass but he wore me out. We dried ourselves and then off to Waffle house he went, to pick us up some grub. I couldn't believe what had just happened, I had this grin on my face that wouldn't go away. I sat there and thought "life is so good right now."

Not even five minutes later it was a knock on the door. I quickly opened it.

"Okay what did you ..." I stopped mid-sentence.

It was Harris, my ex, the one who gave me HIV.

"Merry Christmas baby," he said.

"What the fuck are you doing here, Harris?"

"I want an apology. You know, the one you forgot to give me." Harris said.

"Nigga your drunk, an apology for what?" I replied.

"For how you played me and left after you found out".

"It's been over a year and you show up on this shit now, nigga I am the way I am because of you," I screamed.

"Nobody forced you to open your legs BITCH." Harris yelled.

I was pissed, my eyes turned blood shot red as they began to fill with tears. Did this asshole really just come to my door with this shit and say that to me? I instantly went back to that dark place, the place I fought so hard to escape from. The moment when I found out I was HIV positive. How could the man I thought I loved talk to me in this way, maybe it wasn't love after all.

I ran into the kitchen as Harris followed. He came up from behind me and started to hold me. Everything happened so fast, and all I could see was red! I blacked completely out and grabbed a butcher knife from off the counter, everything went black and then it happened.

I quickly turned around and stabbed him twisting the knife deep in his side, He yelled out and tried to fight me off, but I wanted him to hurt so I pushed it in harder. I wanted him to feel the same pain that I felt when he left me alone to deal with my illnesses. I wanted him dead! We locked eyes one last time as he fell to the floor. I slide down to the floor next to him and yelled "Don't Cry Now, Don't Cry... Motha-Fuckah"

Chapter Five

"Boys Will Be Boys"

My imagination got the best of me, Harris was still behind me and I could still see the butcher knife on the kitchen counter. To my surprise there wasn't even a spot of blood anywhere, I had imagined it all. I wanted to grab it so bad, I really wanted to end his life but I couldn't. I can't believe that I imagined it all, but I just couldn't. I came to the conclusion that I had too much to lose.

"Get off of me, Let me go Harris…" I yelled out, as the front door swung open. Harris quickly let me go and we both looked towards the door. Christopher entered

"What the fuck is this" yelled Christopher.

"Who the fuck are you" said Harris.

"Harris get the fuck out" I yelled.

It was a whole lot of F Bombs being dropped at this moment! My ears were ringing and I never heard Christopher curse since I've known him.

"Oh you're that one nigga" said Christopher.

"Yup, it's me and Daddy's home" yelled Harris.

My mouth dropped to the floor in disbelief, and in the blink of an eye Harris went down from a hard ass blow to the face. The sound of his body hitting the floor was loud as fuck.

"Get up Nigga, I ain't finished with yo bitch ass" Christopher yelled.

Harris was far from a slouch. He quickly rushed to his feet, and ran into the direction of Christopher. Harris tackled Christopher, smashing him into my wooden table, it soon toppled over causing the entire room to shake.

My small apartment was being ruined before my eyes.

Harris was on top of Christopher hitting him with numerous hits to the face, blood was everywhere. So much blood until I couldn't even tell who was bleeding, and who to help.

I yelled out "Stop.. Stop", so much emotion was being thrown around and neither one of them were listening to me. I just couldn't believe that two grown ass men, were standing in front of me fighting like wild animals.

I blinked my eyes and Christopher was on top of Harris with his fist pounding his face in. Harris was heavily intoxicated, but Christopher didn't care, he continued to beat Harris to a bloody pulp. I wondered how this would've turned out if Harris was sober and in his right state of mind.

I pulled Christopher off of Harris, Christopher hugged me and asked me if I was okay. His eyes were blood shot red, full of anger. He was so concerned about me, this man loves me so much and I knew it. I hugged him, and said "Yes baby, I'm okay." I quickly grabbed a towel and wiped Christopher's bloody lip, it was swollen from the fight.

Harris just laid in the middle of the floor grunting from the pain. Moments later Christopher yells "This nigga gotta go."

I suddenly replied "He's drunk Christopher, where is he gonna go in this state, this late at night"

"I don't know, I don't care but he can't stay here" said Christopher.

Christopher's phone began to ring, he answered. Something was wrong I could tell by the expression on his face. He hung up the phone and looked at me, I knew it had something to do with his mother. I said "go Christopher go be with her, your mother needs you." Christopher was just about to say something, but I was so caught up in the moment that I interrupted him. Right in that instance I looked at him and said "Don't worry he will be gone first thing in the morning."

Harris was out for the count, so I told Christopher "that he could stay on the floor for all I cared."

"I'm going to bed and call me as soon as you can. Keep me posted " I told Christopher as he walked out the door.

I could tell by the look on his face that he didn't want to leave but he knew he had to. He kissed me on my forehead and said "Okay, baby I love you." I replied the same as I watched him walk into the night.

I looked down at Harris. "Get up dick head, and get on the couch", I said. He still couldn't walk, so I helped him up and led him to the couch. He smelled as if liquor was gushing out from his pores. He was a complete mess and at this point I'm more annoyed than ever.

He reeked so bad, "YUCK go take a shower, towels are below the sink" I yelled out at him.

He got up, looked at me and said, "I'm sorry for everything I did to you, and how I hurt you. I'm even sorry for the lies, but I can't apologize for still loving you. I'm not the person that I use to be, and I know you love me too because you didn't kick me out."

After saying all of that he moseyed his way to the bathroom. It's amazing that all this time, all I ever really wanted was an apology from him, and I finally got what I wanted and I was still unsatisfied. I thought an apology would make it all better. Silly me I thought to myself, but "I'm sorry" are just words and nothing more.

As he walked away I yelled across the room, "Hey Harris" he turned around and looked at me. I looked him dead in his eyes and said "Fuck You."

Harris just shook his head and continued to walk in the bathroom. I went back into the other room and grabbed his jacket, as I proceeded to hang it up a DVD fell out of his pocket. Me being me, I picked it up to see what it was, and it was The Lion King. I remembered how every time we would argue he would put this movie on, because he knew how much I loved it and I could never be mad and watch The Lion King at the same time. I giggled to myself and began to reminisce and to my surprise my heart began to warm up again. As I closed my eyes, all I could think about was what life was like with Harris O'Neal.

Chapter Six

"Remembering The Past"

It was around 6 o'clock in the evening and I was on summer break from college. I walked through the door of his apartment, I had a spare key just in case of an emergency. Something about this place made me feel at home. You see I spent so much of my time over here, it became my second home. I really didn't talk to my family nor did they accept me because of my homosexuality. Harris was the only family I knew. I proceeded to walk through his apartment and into the bedroom, I took off my clothes and laid down. I was so comfortable and at peace.

I could just smell his scent all over the bed and I loved every bit of it. I looked out of the window and watched the leaves as they fell from the trees. I thought to myself this is home, this is what I want. I didn't want to think about any of the bad, I just wanted to focus on all of the good. Harris and I were together for almost three years. I thought to myself two years off and on, but we are finally here. I dosed off envisioning him holding me tight, as I lay in his bed day became night.

I awoke to the aroma of lasagna and I knew it was his famous homemade dish. Harris enjoyed cooking and I enjoyed eating. I opened my eyes and there he was standing in front of me. He was just standing there watching me sleep, and long enough to watch me wake up. Just imagine waking up to a 5'10 light skinned brutha, with the build of a football player. I was infatuated with his body, and that curly brown hair with those deep dark brown eyes. He was mixed with both Black and Mexican, a 32 year old Gemini with a slick ass mouth and I loved it, I loved everything about him. He definitely had two sides, but he was all I ever knew and I was in love with Harris O'Neal.

"Happy Birthday sleepy head. I came back from my business trip from Atlanta just in time and guess what. I made you some dinner for your big night tonight" said Harris.

"Thank you, I can't believe I'm turning 22" I replied.

"Your still a baby", but your my baby, and I'm going to take care of you" said Harris.

With a look of delight I replied "Forever?" Harris looked at me with a grin of reassurance and said "As long as you want me to."

Dinner was incredible, homemade lasagna, fresh Caesar salad, garlic bread and he topped it off with homemade apple pie with vanilla ice cream.

His voice full of excitement, Harris said "Okay baby go take your shower, we have to head out for your birthday."

I had my own personal dresser at his apartment, I walked in the room and grabbed my outfit for the night. I was so pumped, I walked into the bathroom, turned the shower on, took off my clothes and stepped in. I started to hear music coming from outside the bathroom door, and then suddenly the door opened. Harris pulled back the shower curtain and there he stood, fully naked! He had taken his clothes off and the lights were completely on, for some reason he liked to have sex with the lights on. He loved to see every inch of my body while he fucked me. I looked into his eyes, he began to lick his lips. Every kiss and every touch was filled with passion, I just couldn't get enough.

"I'm still hungry" Harris said, "and there's so much shit I want to do to you, right now."

I looked down at his thick rock hard dick. 10 inches of meat that I couldn't wait to put all in my mouth. "Don't say shit. Turn ya little ass around. Hands on the wall and spread em" commanded Harris. He stepped in the shower and started to kiss down my back. I felt his tongue as he went in and out of my dripping wet hole.

"Damn Baby, you taste so good" said Harris

"Eat up Nigga" I said.

He couldn't wait any longer to see how I felt on the inside. He instantly got up and started to slide his big dick inside of me.

"Let me take my time, I want you to feel every inch as I put this dick inside of you" said Harris.

My mouth opened wide as he slowly entered me and I took it, I wanted it. I needed it. I felt the warm water dripping all over my face as he went deeper inside of me. I gasped for air and when he was all in, all I could say was "Fuck me!!!"

The music stopped and all I could hear was the sound of clapping echoing off the bathroom walls. The harder he fucked me the louder the echo became. It was so intense every time we made love. There were puddles of water all over the bathroom floor.

"You like dis dick Damien…Tell me you like dis dick, tell me you want it harder." moaned Harris

Harder, Harder I screamed out FUCK ME PROPER!

He turned me around and started to kiss me, then up in the air I went. I felt his chest pressed against mine as I wrapped my legs around his waist. Water was dripping down our faces as he fucked me on the shower wall.

"Those other boys you use to mess with don't get it, like I get it, I know how you like it, and I know how you want it baby boy" this ass is mine Harris whispered in my ear.

I moaned out in pure ecstasy, "That's it baby, that's it, I feel it."

His dick throbbing inside of me with every pump, he was so rough and I liked it rough!

"Damn this some good ass baby, I'm never letting you go" said Harris.

He then placed me on the bottom of the bathtub floor, he stuck it back in as I laid on my back. He started choking me and I thought to myself "DAMN, I ain't never had it like this before.

Before I knew it he was moaning "Damn Baby, Damn Damien, What's My Name" said Harris

I whispered "Daddy"

"LOUDER" he said.

I moaned out "DADDY"

"I'm about to nut" he yelled.

He started to shake inside of me and while he shook, I stroked my dick nutting all over myself.

We both exhaled and looked into each other's eyes, "that was the best shower I had ever taken in my entire life", I said out loud.

Harris and I both looked at each other and laughed.

"You can get dis dick in the shower, whenever or wherever you want it baby. You know I'll tare that ass up any and everywhere. Let's finish washing up then we have to head out to the club." said Harris

Chapter Seven

"Fight For Your Life"

I was all dressed and ready to go, the club was 30 minutes away from his place. It was 25 and up but somehow he managed to get me in. I really didn't want to go because none of my friends could get in, but he wanted me to go so I went anyway. Club Illusion was supposed to be the hot spot from what he said. Plenty of attractive older men filled the club and all eyes were on us.

"Harris why does it seem like everyone is staring at us" I asked.

"I never go to the club with anyone on my arm and I want everyone to know were together. They're shocked baby boy, so let them look and admire your sexy ass" said Harris.

Two dudes were looking at us in particular and they both looked my age. One was chunky with dyed bleach blonde hair, with an extra small red shirt on. He had one of the fattest asses I had ever seen on a boy. I guess dudes would love that, but it wasn't for me. The boy really wasn't attractive at all. His face was all twisted up, gave me the impression that he had diarrhea. I remember back in the day when B.E.T after dark would come on and a music video called Tip Drill aired "Must be the ass because it aint yo face" those lyrics definitely applied to this boy. He was standing next to a light skin boy whose neck was missing, so you might as well call him "Benzino" from love and hip hop. Benzino and Winnie the Pooh I thought to myself as I giggled.

I noticed both of them were giving me dirty looks throughout the night, so it made me dance more and more seductive. I danced a little bit harder than usual and giggled a little bit louder. If they wanted a show, I could give a hell of a good show I thought to myself. I had a pretty bad feeling about those two, but the drinks continued to come. It was my birthday and I was not about to pay these hoes any more attention. I was having a good time, and boy did time fly by. All those drinks were finally catching up to me and I had to use the bathroom, so I let Harris know.

"You want me to come with you baby boy", said Harris

"No, I'm a big boy" I replied

"If you're not out in 5 minutes, Daddy is coming in after you" said Harris

"Yeah, Whatever Daddy" I said as I gave him the side eye. Now he knows I do not play that "Daddy" mess in public.

I walked into the bathroom and the same random boy in that too small tight red shirt, and the Benzino look-a-like followed behind me.

I was tipsy and I had this strange feeling in my gut, as if something was about to happen. As soon as I got done, I washed my hands, turned around and there stood Winnie and Benzino directly in front of me.

"While you trying to look all cute in the club you need to be worried about your man and what he's doing when he's on those business trips in Atlanta" said Winnie the Pooh.

"I'm sorry, I know you how? I replied.

"ATL all day Shawty, and naw you don't know me but you can get to know me, just like Harris did last weekend" He yelled out.

I was appalled and in complete shock, how dare this basic ass bitch step to me like this on my birthday. I'm "Damien Hill" I thought to myself.

I said "Oh, well since your from ATL maybe you need to stay there. We have enough THOTS in FLordia already. HOE."

The other boys in the bathroom gasped and their messy asses began to gather around.

"And another thing Pooh Bear, you need to be worried about that too small ass shirt you got on with your nasty ass gut coming out" I yelled.

I'm from the suburbs, and honestly I rarely even curse or use made up words like THOT. Yeah my mouth was lethal, but my hands weren't. I am far from a fighter, and I've never been in this type of situation before, but I was so pissed and drunk in love like Yonce. So before he could utter another word, I heard a voice say Damien smack this disrespectful ass hoe.

So I listened to that voice and I smacked that hoe.

I don't think I should've done that because before I knew it I was on the floor and Pooh bear was on top of me whooping my ass.

"Somebody get this fat bitch off of me" I yelled out.

Then Benzino no neck ass jumped in and started stomping me.

Okay so the boy name is not Benzino but that's what we are going to call him. I was out done, I really had no idea what was going on.

Harris ran in the bathroom and tackled the boy that was stomping me. After Harris tackled the Benzino, He instantly yoked the other one up and threw him into the bathroom mirror causing it to shatter everywhere. Security rushed in but they were too late.

The bathroom was rocking and I was the center of attention. It was blood from my mouth all on my white custom made hoody that fitted me to perfection.

The boy yelled out "how could you Harris."

Harris repeatedly punched the boy in the face and he started leaking blood. I was still in shock.

Harris yelled out "you trying to fuck up my shit Rico."

Security finally grabbed Harris, but he was so enraged that he started fighting security. Harris was a boxer and he knew how to fight. Mace was sprayed and everyone ran out of the bathroom. Security grabbed me and the next thing I knew Harris was in handcuffs being escorted outside. I was trying to explain to the police how I was attacked but Harris was going crazy right into the backseat of the police car. I was like a deer in head lights. I couldn't move.

"Call my boss Damien, Let him know what happened" Harris yelled out from the car.

I had Harris phone and car keys. I watched as the police drove him off. I immediately called his boss and explained to him what happened, his boss assured me that he would be out tomorrow morning. Harris worked for a law firm.

Ironic right? but it was his family's business. I drove back to Harris house in disbelief of the night's events. I pulled up at his house and ran to the shower. I watched as the blood ran from my mouth into the tub. I was in pain and I just wanted Harris home with me.

After the shower I laid in his bed with the phone next to me. I started to think back to what Winnie said to Harris. Then it hit me, wait a minute, they knew each other. I grabbed Harris phone. Then I put it back. I can't, I won't, and I trust this man.

Then that little voice inside my head said "Don't be a stupid hoe, you better go through phone" and I proceeded to go through it.

Yes I did, and there were messages on top of messages, all these ass pictures were in his phone. Messages about meeting up, and how he liked it RAW? My mouth was wide open, I was shocked at what I was reading. My eyes filled up with water. Wow, what a great birthday surprise. I laid in his bed and cried myself to sleep.

Chapter Eight

"Life Or Death"

I woke up early the next morning to his phone ringing. I knew it was him calling from jail. He got the wrong one I thought to myself. I called my roommate Lee to come pick me up. I explained everything that happened to my roommate.

I was sad and I felt so lost inside. You know when you're with someone for years, and you think this is finally it, this is who I am going to be with. I just knew it. That's how I felt about Harris. He was the one for me or at least that's what I thought. I was attending college away from my family and that's how I wanted it to be, as far away from them as possible. Don't get me wrong my family loved me dearly, but hated the fact that I was homosexual. I needed love and that's what Harris provided me with. He gave me that love. The love I felt I needed. We had spent every holiday together. How could he do this to me, I thought to myself. How could he do this to us? Better yet, how could I be so dumb?

Days went past and I heard nothing from Harris. Days turned into weeks and weeks turned into months. He went m.i.a. on me and I missed him, I did but I have to be smart. I was focused on my school work and refused to think about Harris and then it happened.

It was a Friday night, well early Saturday morning and I was walking out of my on campus apartment to head to the little store next door and there he was walking towards his car. My heart dropped, I was surprised and I wanted to know why he was here? Was he looking for me?

Then Riley Smith walked past me, he was known as the whore with the dreadlocks that magically grew over night. Riley's apartment was right across the hall from me and he stayed having all different types of men coming in and out of his room. Better yet we can say cum'n in and out of him, so I knew Harris couldn't have been leaving his room at 12:30 am. Well at least that's what I thought. I guess I was still a little delusional.

I walked up to Riley and said "Excuse me hun, How do you know Harris?"

In my head I'm thinking I really don't want to have to fuck this bitch up knowing good and damn well I can't fight.

"Um, Damien, right? You don't know me enough to ask me what I do and WHO I'm DOING" said Riley with a smirk on his face.

"You and your judgmental ass need to stay out of my business, walking around campus like you're so sweet and all suburban. Girl bye. I see right through you" said Riley.

Then it happened again, that same voice popped up in my head and said "Damien smack this disrespectful ass hoe."

Riley turned his back on me and kept walking. I jumped on his ass like a speeding bullet and I didn't smack that hoe, I tackled that hoe.

Oh yeah! Ya boy Damien learned some new tricks. I watched enough wrestling, JLO from that movie Enough, and Bad Girls Club to know how to whoop some ass now.

We both got up off the ground, I start swinging and I mean I'm landing all type of hits. This hoe is fucking my man, I have to beat his ass I thought to myself.

Then Riley got that one good hit on me, straight dead in my face. Everything went black for a minute and during a fight a lot can happen in a minute.

Next thing I know, I'm on my back getting my ass whooped. Not again I thought to myself, Natalie Nunn, Jennifer Lopez, and the ROCK, you all have failed me.

Someone started pulling Riley off of me but I wasn't finished with that little hoe yet. While Riley was getting pulled off of me, I grabbed him by his little dreadlocks or whatever that fuzzy shit was in his head and proceeded to pull.

"You fucking with my man bitch" I yelled out.

"Let go of my hair you crazy fag" screamed Riley.

"What the fuck are you doing, let go" screamed Harris.

"You fucking this nasty bitch", I yelled at Harris while yanking Riley around by his fake ass synthetic hair. I finally let his hair go and snatched out a large patch of that fake shit.

"You are crazy, we are on campus, what if someone would've saw us. We would both be up for expulsion. You two can have each other" Riley said while storming off.

"Baby, you are crazy", Harris said with laughter while hugging me.

I pushed Harris off of me, I was drained mentally and physically. I knew Harris wasn't good for me. I ran back into my dorm. I heard him yell out for me but I ignored his yelling. I finally got in my room and by then my phone kept ringing. I knew it was him and I didn't want to answer, so I didn't answer. Then text after text, I love you, I miss you, and baby let's talk, were all the messages flashing on my iPhone.

I took a moment and looked in the mirror and I began to cry, I looked thin, I looked different. I couldn't recognize myself. Who was this person Damien was becoming, I never cursed so much in my life. I wasn't reading the bible or anything. I needed church and I had no one to turn to but God. The following Sunday night I decided to get my life back in order and try to get back to the old Damien. I wanted to be the man I was before I met Harris. Prayer was the only answer, so I kneeled down and prayed.

"You have been lord Jesus and you will be. You have always been in my life Oh father and I have lost my way. You know when I sleep and slumber, you know my heart Jesus. You keep your angels around me and you cover me with your love. I come to you tonight Lord Jesus asking you for your forgiveness. You have saved my life so many times before and I am grateful. Tonight I am asking you for clarity and guidance for my heart is broke and I feel weak. Please open my eyes lord, please give me the knowledge and the strength I need to keep moving forward. You know every detail of my life, please help me Jesus. Please help me father, you are God and you don't miss a thing."

"You know me Jesus" I cried out.

"You know my heart Jesus" I cried out.

"Help me God."

"Please help me Jesus" I yelled as tears began to fall out of my eyes.

Monday had come and it was national HIV awareness day and I figured why not get tested. I want a fresh start, I want to make sure everything is alright with me and I'm going to church service tonight. I went to the doctor right before the clinic was going to close. I was a little nervous but I was calm and I felt like I'd be fine. I was experiencing night sweats but I didn't think too much of it. The doctor came in the room with a straight face. I smiled because deep down inside I already knew my results.

"Damien Hill, Your are HIV Positive."

I smiled and shook my head. Everything else that came out his mouth was noise. I got up and proceeded to walk out the room. The Doctor grabbed me, I moved his hands and walked out of the clinic. It seemed to be getting dark and the parking lot was nearly empty. I felt like a zombie, simply lifeless. Somehow I just began to walk, where I was walking to, I had no idea.

It's like everything was happening in slow motion. I finally stopped walking and I didn't get far. I looked up at the sky and I felt a wet drizzle on my face. I couldn't tell my tears from the rain drops. I whispered why God and then it hit me. In that moment I realized my life will never be the same. I am forever changed. I felt heavy, my heart filled with pain and grief. How could I have been so stupid? I blamed myself. I let this man bring me down to hell and now I can't find my way out.

I Screamed, and I screamed "I hate you, I hate you."

"I HATE ME" I yelled.

My screams were full of hurt and filled with pain.

Then I thought to myself, God answered my prayers. I needed to know this. I needed to know what was going on with me. This wasn't the end, this is just the beginning. I could be dead laid out somewhere, walking around not knowing, or continue being with Harris getting played as my health continued to deteriorate. The signs were there but I chose to ignore them. God wouldn't put too much on us that we cannot bare, and even with that thought in my head,I wasn't thinking about how blessed I was or how blessed I will be.

I was becoming dizzy and I couldn't breathe. It began to rain harder. The cold drops hit my body non-stop. I grabbed my heart and fell to the floor and in the moment I would've gladly died. All I felt was pain and I wanted it. I welcomed death. Yes, sweet suburban Damien Hill wished for death.

The nurses and the doctor ran outside the small clinic as I began to shake on the ground. Breathe they said, Breathe the doctor yelled. I imagined Harris holding me and everything went black. The messed up part about it is, I still loved him.

Chapter Nine

"Good Bye Forever "

The bathroom door opened and awoke me from my flash back. The scent of my dove soap filled the front room. Harris walked up and set beside me on the couch.

"Baby what's wrong, your eyes are blood shot red" said Harris.

"Nigga do not and I repeat do not call me baby." I said.

"Damien, talk to me, what's wrong", said Harris.

"What's wrong is that you showed up at my door out of nowhere.

What's wrong is that you hurt me like no one has ever hurt me Before. What's wrong is that you gave me HIV. What's wrong is that you made me fall in love with you and then you turned your back on me."

I tried to be strong but I couldn't hold back the tears.

"Damien I am sorry, I am a changed man and I am here to prove it. I love you baby boy, I never stopped loving you. I was confused, I was trifling. Hell I didn't even know I had HIV, and if I'd known I would've never."

I interrupted him before he could finish.

"You said you cared about me, love me, and that you would always be there for me."

Harris looked down and tears began to fall from his eyes

"Look at me I yelled. Don't cry for me because I don't want your tears, I am happy. I am in love, in love with a man who knows the real me. A man who is honest. A man who didn't try to ruin my life. You were supposed to be my fairy tale but you were nothing but a night mare."

"If you want me to leave Damien I will leave, but I swear I will never stop loving you" said Harris.

"Good bye Harris" I said as I pointed toward the door. I watched as Harris wiped his tears and grabbed his things. As he stopped in the middle of the door way, he looked back and said

"Damien I will be sending you money for the table and the damages to your place"

"Good" I said.

"Oh and one more thing Damien"

What's that Harris?

"I'll be back."

I jumped as the door slammed shut. He'll be back. What the hell does that mean? I thought to myself. I locked the door and went into my bedroom. So many thoughts, emotions and memories all flooded my mind as I laid in bed praying that sleep would somehow find me.

3 Months later

Still no sign of Harris and I thank God for that, hopefully he went back to the gutter he crawled out of. I still have so much resentment towards him in my heart but in church

I've learned in order to continue to receive God's blessings you must first forgive. Have I forgiven Harris? No, but I'm a work in progress. Everything is going great with Christopher and me. I truly love him.

"Um Mr. Hill, Are you day dreaming, I'm waiting for your answer" said Professor Maxwell.

Here we go again, I thought to myself. I am in Pop Culture Two with this same dumb Professor. I can never catch a break with him.

"Well Professor, I believe that in today's society within pop culture anything goes. It's all about that shock factor like it's been before. Your nothing without some type of scandal" I said.

"By the way has anyone been watching scandal? because Olivia Pope is the truth."

The class laughed, even Professor Maxwell chuckled which shocked the hell out of me.

Professor Maxwell stood 6'1 Latino and black. He has a chunky football player built. He had brown hair with beautiful skin, I always wanted to ask him about his skin care products. It was clear that he was part of the family meaning gay. Professor Maxwell had to be about 32 and extremely attractive but I was not interested in him and I knew he had the least bit of interest in me. I wondered if he was a queen, but by his mannerisms he seemed very masculine. One man's top is another man's bottom and that's probably the case for Professor Maxwell. I'm so mad that I had to take him again this semester.

"Good answer Mr. Hill now let's focus" said Professor Maxwell.

Ugh, I couldn't stand him and then it happened, I looked over and my ex roommate Lee walked into lecture class. There were no seats left in the lecture class besides the one next to yours truly. Lee looked at me, mean mugged me and sat his high yellow ass right next to me. We had a bad falling out over Harris along with other meaningless altercations. Lee never liked him and I didn't listen. I was a boy in love and clearly you couldn't tell me anything about my man. I should've listened, but Lee definitely played his part behind the reasons we fell out.

We were both very young but now we are older and I missed his friendship dearly. I decided to write him a note during class. I was in a happy space and his friendship would just add to my happiness. I wrote on a piece of paper Friend Contract. Will you be my friend again? Check yes or NAH.. I passed it to him during class. He marked on it, folded it up and handed it to me. I read the note and to my dismay he checked NAH and put still childish I see. I couldn't help but to laugh, I knew Lee had a messed up attitude but damn can he give me a break.

"UM Mr. Hill, Lee Johnson do you guys want to share with the rest of the class what you two are passing notes about like little school girls". Said Professor Maxwell

"Excuse me" Lee said.

"You heard me" said Professor Maxwell.

All eyes were on us as Professor Maxwell waited for his answer. I thought to myself "oh no he didn't."

I replied "well Professor if you insist on knowing"

"Oh GOD" Lee said out loud

"I really just want that old thing back and I miss that stroke" I said with a straight face.

A majority of dudes in the lecture class looked disgusted. One even yelled out "Aw hell naw." while the ladies said "aww" and whomever else wasn't commenting laughed. The class was in an uproar and I sat there smiling while Lee laughed. He looked at me and smiled. Just like old times. Lee already knew how I would respond, we've known each other for a long time

"Settle down, I'll see you after class Mr. Hill" said Professor Maxwell.

Class is finally over and it was time for me to receive my punishment for my actions in class.

"Look Damien, I think you're a bright kid but the decisions that you make in class are not the best. You came to class late all last semester, and now you're in class passing notes and day dreaming. Also the class doesn't need to know about your sexual preference Mr. Hill. I need you to pull it together or our next conversation will not be so nice. Do you understand me Mr. Hill" said Professor Maxwell.

"Yes I understand" I said.

"Good because I expect more from you, I see so much potential in you Damien. I love your work so let's just focus and if you need to talk to me about anything my office door is open. Now go and play or something" said Professor Maxwell

"Oh Ge wilikers, thanks Professor Maxwell" I chuckled.

"Cut the sarcasm Mr. Hill, I apologize for saying go play."

I walked out of the lecture hall so thankful to be out of there and to my surprise Lee was outside waiting for me.

"So how did it go" he said.

"I'm still alive" I said, and we both laughed.

"I missed you Damien" said Lee.

I told Lee" I missed him as well, friends again" I said

"Yeah, friends again" he replied.

We spent that whole afternoon catching up. Time passed by so fast, I didn't even notice that Christopher hadn't called me all day. So after me and Lee caught up, I went back to my place and called Christopher.

Chapter Ten

"Another Heart Break"

I hadn't heard from Christopher in a couple of days which was very odd. He wasn't even answering my phone calls. I knew his mother was getting worst but damn, I really missed him. I've been calling him all damn day and finally he answers.

"Umm Hello, where have you been Mister "I said playfully.

"My mother hasn't been well and she wants to go back to Cleveland Clinic said Christopher.

"So what does that mean Christopher?"

"That means I am leaving. I will not put you or anyone before my mother." said Christopher

"DAMN, Christopher I understand that but are you seriously telling me this stuff over the phone."

"I'm on the way" he said hanging up in my ear.

I thought to myself, are you fucking serious right now? Everything has been going so well. I am finally happy and then he pulls some shit like this. He wasn't even going to call me, I had to call him. I was pissed and I couldn't fathom the thought of him leaving me. 30 minutes had passed and I was even more pissed. If I was a cartoon steam would be flowing from my ears.

Christopher walked into my door, he walked past me and sat on the couch. So I went sat right next to him, for some weird reason he couldn't look me in my face.

"Look at me Christopher, what's going on with you? Just talk to me please" I said.

"Im moving back to Cleveland, you know my mother's health has always been an issue and now it's so severe that we need to go back" said Christopher.

"Wait so how long have you known this? You've been making plans to move back to Cleveland, is that the reason why you're not enrolled in school right now? You're moving back there and you've known this for months haven't you?"

"It's true, I can never lie to you Damien. I love you but I have to support my mother and what she wants to do. Damien she may be on her death bed. I have to go with my mother. Do you know how hard it has been looking you in your eyes and keeping this from you? I don't even know how to talk to you about this, about leaving you." said Christopher.

"Leaving me, wait are you breaking up with me Christopher? I said

"Your eyes are getting red, baby that's not what I said Damien"

"What the fuck is it Christopher?

"It's, a break baby. That's all it is, I'm not sure how long I will be in Cleveland but I know that I'll be back for you. So yes, we're breaking up only because we have to. I don't believe in long distance and neither do you. So let's just slow it down and I'll be back."

I felt like all the windows were shattering in my house at once. It was some supernatural shit going on and I wasn't here for it. I was so pissed, I couldn't even think straight.

"Well what if you go back there and find a normal boy, a boy without..."

"Without what Damien? Without HIV, are you serious right now Damien? You are normal. Damien you still don't realize your worth do you. How unique, how special you are. You never asked for HIV, it's something that happened, something that was given to you. You're still normal, you're beautiful and I love you" Christopher said as he wiped my eyes.

I knew he meant it, but how could the love of my life just leave me like this. I really didn't know what to think. I don't mean to be selfish but I'm finally happy.

"When are you leaving Christopher", I whispered.

"Tomorrow baby he said in a soft voice"

"GET THE FUCK OUT" I screamed.

I jumped up and ran towards the door, I proceeded to open it, so that he can make his exit. Christopher ran towards me and shut the door before I could fully open it. He grabbed me by my shoulders and made me look him straight in the eye.

"I love you baby, I never would intentionally hurt you" said Christopher.

He picked me up like a baby and carried me into the bedroom.

"I'm not a baby" I said.

He then dropped me on the bed which made me giggle. He jumped in the bed next to me. I pushed him away.

"So is this our last night together" I whispered.

He began to softly kiss me on my lips.

"No, tonight is not our last night together, I will call you all the time, we can Face Time, we'll talk baby. This is just one bridge that we are going to have to cross and we'll cross it together" Christopher said.

Tears started to roll down my face. I still wasn't exactly sure what was happening right now.

"Don't cry baby", he said as he held me tight. I loved the way he would hold me. Christopher's touch literally made me feel like I was the only boy in the world. His voice was always so calming to my soul, I can't believe this was the boy I couldn't stand months ago and now he's breaking my heart.

I fell asleep in his arms that night. He never let me go, we never changed positions. I held onto him like it was our last night together. Little did I know that would be the last night. That would be the last time I would ever see him face to face or feel his touch.

In the blink of an eye it was morning and Christopher was kissing me goodbye. He fought back the tears as mine just rolled. He was leaving me and I understood that he had too, so I let him go. He's such a loving man and at that time I thought he would be back for me so I let him leave my side but I'll never let him leave my heart.

The next month would be a hard one for me, I was single again and this time I felt alone. Being with Christopher was amazing I was getting healthier by the day. He always had me eating healthy and working out with him. Now that he's gone, I haven't really been feeling like doing anything except for slouching around and making Lee watch chick flicks with me. I talked to Christopher off and on throughout the month. His mother was getting better but he was growing distant and I knew I wasn't making it any better. I couldn't comfort him or be there for him like I should. Hell, I couldn't even be there for myself. I need to have some fun according to Lee and this Friday night was supposed to be one to remember Lee proclaimed. Lee was always getting me in some mess so I didn't know what to expect.

Chapter Eleven

"Time To Party"

I put on my go-get-him outfit, which really means a black fitted V-neck shirt, to show off my little muscles and some thin leg jeans, not to be confused with skinny jeans and some bomb ass kicks. Since my outfit was so simple I had to let my shoes and accessories do the talking. I heard knocks at my door, I could hear Lee's crazy ass yelling on the other end. I peeked through the peep hole and he looked stunning. Lee believed every time we step out, we need to let the gays know Hunnie, we are here.

Lee is so extra and I love it, he wore a tight red blazer with black leather pants and some hot ass red kicks. Lee was with this guy named Rucker. Rucker was a little fast, Okay ...so yeah, Rucker was a buss it wide open hoe.

He had a serious reputation for fucking everyone, tops, bottoms, and females. There was no hole too small or no dick too big that Rucker couldn't handle. He was true life THOT as some would say. Thot stands for That or Them Hoes Over There depending on how you use it. Our generation and the words they make up, but anyways. I was a little confused why Lee would show up with Rucker.

"Open the door BEOTCH, I know your depressed skinny ass is in there you little cute Twig you" Lee playfully said.

I opened the door and Lee eyes lit up. "You look cute as fuck bitch, you ready" said Lee. I laughed and said "yesssss!" Lee use to always give off this trade look, meaning he looks like a straight boy/man or whatever you want to call it, he gave it. People would often think we were together but that was my BFF and I'm so glad I have him back in my life. He knew all of my darkest secrets and never judged me. Wow, times have really changed us. I watched him blossom from the trade into a fashionista. He wears everything from crop tops to basketball shorts and the men loved it and so did the ladies.

"Hey Damien boo, you ready for tonight" Rucker said.

A look of confusion came over my face. I still couldn't believe Rucker was in my apartment.

Lee interrupted and said "enough small talk, I need some cologne" which was our code for go into your room, I have some tea for you and company can't hear.

I laughed to myself because I already knew we were on the same page. "Okay follow me Lee" I said.

Lee followed me into my bedroom

"Okay Damien, Bitch don't look at me like that, Rucker is cool" Lee said.

"Rucker is a hoe, Lee and you know it" I said with laughter.

"Yeah, but this hoe be knowing where the hottest parties are so let's roll, live Damien and have some fun. You have this whole suburban Cinderella, crazy damsel in distress bull shit going on. You only live once. So please make the most of it" Lee said.

Lee and those damn pep talks, gets me every time, so off we went.

The car ride was taking forever and I was becoming extremely impatient.

"Rucker, tell me about this house party" I said.

"Okay, so it's like a mix and mingle type of ordeal. It's going to be full of older men between the ages of 25 to 45. If you're looking for stability with a rock hard dick then this is the spot" said Rucker.

"Sounds like a party" screamed Lee, as he passed a me a water bottle filled with liquor.

We pulled up into this huge driveway, big enough to park about ten cars in the front and even more in the back. We all got out the car and looked at the Mansion and said "DAYUM." I high fived Lee and by this time we were both good and tipsy. This is going to be an interesting night. I just want to flirt and twerk and twerk and flirt. Okay well less twerking and more flirting. I really think this should be a mature little mingle session. Secretly though I'd rather be home cuddled up under Christopher but he's gone now so I have to live my life.

We walked into the dim lite house, and it was full of men. What I couldn't understand is why the vibe was so sexual. This house party wasn't at all what I expected. It was sex toys everywhere, but who cares, this house was laid out. Everywhere I turned there was a flat screen television, fish tanks, fur rugs, tons of bedrooms and bathrooms.

When we walked into the main room it looked as if all the younger men were on the right and the older were on the left. The owner of the house made his way down stairs, he stopped and looked at all three of us with a huge devilish smile on his face.

We have babies in the house, "The Young Sickening Bitches" have entered, now the party can really start said the owner.

I laughed, I kind of like the name young sickening bitches. Everyone laughed and started to mingle and socialize. It was so many handsome men, so many sizes, hues, and races. It was like going to Golden Corral, instead of food there were men. I met this dude named Marcus he was so dreamy plus he reminded me of Christopher. The way I was drinking everyone in the room looked like Christopher and after my second long island, hell, I thought I was talking to Christopher. I couldn't fathom why there were so many single men and no couples. It was a little too much for me but hey I was enjoying myself so much, I didn't even notice that Lee and Rucker had disappeared. The music was on point, I heard some Lil' Wayne, Nicki Minaj, they even hit us with some Aaliyah, and you know they had to play Beyonce for the kids. So Beyonce was hitting the speakers all throughout the night!

It had just turned midnight and I overheard some young men talking about how they had to leave before 1:00am. Then another boy chimed in and said "you know what happens here after 1." They laughed and proceeded to leave. I was confused as to what they were talking about. I looked all over for Lee and Rucker but kept getting distracted from dancing and talking, before I knew it 1:00am had hit. The atmosphere and vibe felt totally different than before, the owner of the house was making an announcement.

"It is time to begin our annual Purge" he said with Laughter.

Annual Purge I thought to myself. What the fuck does that mean?

Chapter Twelve

"The Annual Purge"

I looked around the room and the lights became dimmer. Marcus whom I was dancing with started to take off his clothes.

"What are you doing" I asked Marcus.

Marcus looked at me with this puzzled look, then started making out with this random boy that came out of NO WHERE!

I started to look around the room, my eyes became wide and my mouth dropped open in disbelief. I couldn't believe what I was witnessing, there were naked men everywhere. It was so crazy, men were kissing, sucking, fucking you name it.

What did Rucker's ass get us into? I thought to myself. I started to walk through the crowd, and it became darker. I could barely see my hands in front of my face. Someone grabbed my butt, I turned around and it was the host.

"Either you're going to fuck or you're going to get out" the host said as he looked me in my eyes.

I can't believe this, Rucker's' ass dragged us into this damn sex party. I've only heard about these and never experienced it. The Host proceeded to walk closer to me, I was so drunk I stumbled backwards into a bedroom. He walked in the room behind me and closed the door, no one else was in the room from what I could see.

"You want this Dick or you want this Kitty Kat" he said while one hand on my ass and the other on his hard dick. He aggressively pushed me and I fell on the bed hitting my head on the head board. He was way bigger than me and it was all happening so fast. I was dazed from the hard blow to my head. He started to unbuckle my pants and proceeded to pull them down.

"Stop it, Stop" I yelled out as I struggled to pull my pants up.

He was all over me and reeked of alcohol. I felt myself becoming nauseous. I used all of my force pushing him off of me, and his drunk ass fell on the floor.

Like a white girl in a horror flick, I ran out the door. My hair was bouncing and swinging everywhere as I ran, well in my head my hair was bouncing.

"Come back here you little bitch" he yelled.

I was in complete darkness, the only light came from the windows. All I heard was loud moans, and skin smacking skin. I felt like I was surrounded in a pool full of sex. My eyes were still adjusting to the darkness and I still couldn't see. I made eye contact with this young boy who was on the couch getting hit from the back by this older broad shoulder football player built man. The young boy smiled as he moaned, getting louder with every stroke. The older man behind him pulled out and another one entered! The boy smiled and reached out for me to come join. Hell, fuck no! I thought to myself. I was disgusted.

I moved quickly through the crowd whispering Lee's name and then I tripped over something. I looked behind me and it was this hoe Rucker riding some random man. This little whore knew exactly where he was taking us, I knew Lee was not here for this. I stayed close to the wall and still felt nauseous, I needed a bathroom and fast. I twisted knobs walking into different rooms filled with men having sex. I finally ran into the bathroom and closed the door. I flicked the light switch but the light didn't come on.

"Damn, I'm in here" someone said.

"I'm sorry I just need to use my phone real quick so I can get out of here" I replied.

"Take your time, it's just me in here, I'm hiding out. I had no idea what kind of party this was going to be and of course my crew isn't picking up" the familiar voice said.

I looked at my phone, and I had 5 missed calls from Lee and back to back text messages. The last message said "I'm outside where are you? I called my dude to come pick us up, where are you?"

"DAMN" I said out loud.

"Are you okay" said the mysterious voice out of the darkness.

"YES, I need to get out of here immediately" I said. This isn't my cup of tea, I knew I should've stayed my black ass at home."

"Me and you both, look we took two cars and I drove so if you want me to take you home" the familiar voice said.

"Um, I'll pass" I replied. I didn't even know this man I thought to myself.

"I promise, it's not even like that" he said.

"Yeah Okay says the guy at the sex party" I said aloud.

"You're here just like me, but hey if you want to stay here then that's on you. I'm not going to force you to do anything you don't want to do Mr." said the voice.

His voice sounded so familiar and that tone irritated the hell out of me, and then someone started banging on the door.

"Okay, Okay, just get me out of here" I said

The mysterious man, grabbed my hand and swung the door open. I was still very drunk and everything was a little blurry. His hands felt strong, a nice firm grip, I instantly felt safe with him for some odd reason as he led me through the darkness.

"Fuck Me big Daddy" someone yelled.

The mysterious man laughed and we exited through the door running straight into Lee and his dude. It seemed extremely bright outside but it really wasn't, my eyes were still trying to adjust.

The mysterious man's back faced towards me. I looked at Lee and his eyes were wide open like he was looking at a ghost.

"Professor" said Lee.

"Professor" I said in shock.

The mysterious man immediately let my hand go and turned around.

"Wow" he said with a look of disbelief.

I was speechless, shocked and of course still drunk. The mysterious man who led me to safety is the same man who I couldn't stand. It was Professor Maxwell.

"Well I'll let you two handle your business" said Lee as he walked off.

"No, Lee I need a ride home" I said with irritation in my voice.

"You enjoy Professor Maxell" He said with laughter.

"Damien, would you like me to take you home" said Professor Maxwell

"Hell Naw" I said

"Suite yourself" said Professor Maxwell as he walked off.

"Wait, wait, and okay take me with you" I said

I knew Lee was about to go to some afterhours spot and I really needed to go home.

Professor Maxwell drove a Range Rover, I was thoroughly impressed and a little intrigued. I didn't want him to know my address but I gave it to him anyway and then the car ride began. He put on Lauren Hill which was pretty calming especially after a night like this. I can't believe I didn't see him the whole time I was there.

"Damien, if you need extra help with the assignment, I live 15 minutes away, we can meet at Starbucks or something and I'll help you. Just don't mention tonight to your friends and please tell Lee do not say anything" said Professor Maxwell.

"Does this mean I will definitely get my A out of the course" I said jokingly.

Professor Maxwell looked at me and said "you have to earn that A just like you did last semester. You can do it Damien, you're a great student, It's just that you seem dazed and not in tune with the class. You rarely interact and when asked questions during class you seem to get so defensive. I don't understand it and I don't like it."

"Well your always coming at me crazy during class with these random questions, I feel like your attacking me. Also you are very sarcastic when you talk to me Professor Maxwell. It's like your being condescending or something" I replied.

"Well Damien if you didn't think you knew it all" said Professor Maxwell.

"You don't even know me Professor Maxwell, You don't know my life and or what I deal with on a day to day basis and coming to your class started off as an outlet. I actually enjoy listening to you talk. I love your theories but you are irritating as Hell."

"You can call me Jose, and since we're not in the classroom anymore you know what Damien, you look like the type to be like ohhh me, ohhhh my drama' oh my life is horrible. Well guess what Damien this is the real world and everyone has issues."

Professor Maxwell has clearly been drinking and was driving a little crazy. He was so intense and yelling at me while swerving on the road.

"Pay attention to the road" I yelled out.

We pulled up into my driveway and all I can think is how dare he talk to me like this?

"Isn't this your stop" said Professor Maxwell

I slammed the car door and stormed up the stairs. I can't believe his grown ass talking to me like that and to my surprise Professor Maxell, I mean Jose, or whatever the fuck he's calling himself these days was right behind me. I opened my front door and he walked his ass right on in.

"Can I help you" I said

"Damien, I just want to apologize. I'm sorry I've been drinking". He began to stumble.

I ran over to help him to the couch. He grabbed me and began to kiss me.

"Whoa wait, what are you doing", I said as I pushed him off of me.

I'm so sorry Damien, I didn't mean to, I've been drinking and I'm sorry.

I grabbed Professor Maxwell and started kissing him harder. He picked me up and carried me into the kitchen, I wanted him and I wanted it right now. I started to unbuckle his pants and then it hit me. I can't do this, I don't know him outside the class room, he doesn't know me or my situation. So I stopped him again.

What is it Damien? What's wrong, I have protection.

"I just can't, you don't know me" I said.

"I understand you're a baby so I'll just leave" said Professor Maxwell.

I'll show him baby, FUCK IT, I thought to myself. If this is what he wants then I'm going to give it to him.

I immediately dropped to my knees, I slowly looked up at him as he ripped his shirt off. My eyes looking right at his six pack, and that nice firm chest. I proceeded to rub on his abs, I had no idea all this time Professor Maxwell had all this body. He looked down at me and smiled, I then unbuckled his belt releasing his big thick dick. He then grabbed my head and started ramming all of it in my mouth, instantly chocking me.

"Spit on it" said Professor Maxwell, so I did as I was told and he loved it.

"That's a good boy" he said.

He picked me up and put me on the dining room table, he then unbuckled my belt and started sucking me off. I felt my dick throbbing in his mouth, he knew exactly what he was doing. He then raised up and whispered in my ear, I'm gone give you this good dick. He put on the condom and proceeded to slowly slide in me. It hurt so bad but I wanted it, I deserve this dick, I thought to myself. Finally a little bit of fun to ease my heart break. He was kissing me in all the right spots so I wouldn't't focus on the pain. I wanted every inch from 1 to 10 inside of me and I felt him, all of him. He started off slow, but I wanted it harder.

"Fuck me harder" I moaned out.

He went harder, and harder, in and out of me. I started queefing so good. Oh what's queefing you say? Queefing is basically like when a females vagina makes noises from being banged out so good. So yes my ass was queefing, he breathed heavily in my ear and I knew he was about to explode. I finished right behind him. Everything happened so fast, we laid there for about 10 minutes, just looking at the ceiling.

Then he turned me over on the dining room table, spread my legs and I felt his warm tongue in between my ass, he ate me so good. I haven't had this feeling in a long time, I turned around and asked, "Are you sure this is what you want" as I rubbed his hard dick.

"Let me show you what I want" he said "get on all fours", again I did as I was told.

I felt him enter me from the back. "Damn Baby, that ass is so wet" he moaned out. I felt him deep inside of me, our bodies were in perfect harmony. I touched myself as he fucked me, I couldn't help how loud I was and I exploded everywhere. He pulled out took the condom off ... "Damn, Damn" he moaned in my ear as he bust all on my ass and back. He was exhausted and so was I. Then reality hit us both at the same damn time. I just slept with my Professor who earlier today I couldn't stand. There was an awkward silence. He rushed up and put his clothes on.

"I should head home" Professor Maxwell said.

"Yeah, drive safely" I replied.

He kissed me on my forehead and proceeded to walk towards the door, He turned around and looked at me.

"This stays between us" he said.

"Don't worry, I still don't like you" I replied.

We both laughed as he walked out the door. I couldn't believe that had happened, but I'm not going to think about it anymore.

Chapter Thirteen

"Relationship with A Gemini"

It was Monday and I was in Professor Maxwell's class on time. Lee sat next to me and smiled. "Damien, How was your night with the Professor or should I call you Ginger now" playfully said Lee.

We both giggled.

"Hmm, Lets just say Gilligan's island was hit by a tusnami and the Professor saved me over and over gain" I replied. We both started giggling like two little school girls.

"Hush, pay attention" I said.

"Oh, now she wants to pay attention and shit. Professor must've laid that educated grown man dick on ya" Lee said.

I proceeded to ignore Lee and his funny comments, but I really really wanted to laugh.

During class Professor Maxwell and I constantly made eye contact. I kept thinking about him being inside of me and his body, I could barely pay attention to his lecture but I couldn't take my eyes off of him. Class would soon be coming to an end, Professor Maxwell always walked around the room during his speeches, and he stopped at my table.

"Mr. Harris, I need you to come by my office Today."

I shook my head nodding yes, and I could feel Lee, looking at me.

I was finished with all my classes and it was time to go see Professor Maxwell in his office. I was a little nervous, not exactly sure what he wanted to talk about. I walked in and remained standing.

"Hello Damien, have a seat. You're doing great in the class a big improvement."

I sat down. "Thank you Professor Maxwell, but is that what you really wanted to talk to me about? I questioned.

Professor Maxwell got up to close the door.

"No, I want to talk about the other night. I want to apologize for how everything went down. I'm not that kind of man and I."

"Professor Maxwell, it's okay, I understand. We are both adults and we made a conscious decision to have sex, it no longer needs to be discussed." I said before letting him explain.

"But that's the thing Damien it does" said Professor Maxwell.

A puzzled look came across my face.

"You see, I want to get to know you better. I want to take you out on date. Look I have another class to teach in a minute, so tonight Maggiano's 9:00 pm. I'll see you there"

I couldn't believe he was asking me out on a date, and before I could even utter a word, he was out the door. I thought to myself why not, what's to loose. The rest of the day flew by and in the blink of an eye it was time for my date. My nerves were all over the place and I just didn't know what to say or how to act but one thing was for certain, I'm going to have to be honest with him about everything. Another great conversation, I am not looking forward to having.

I met Professor Maxwell at Maggiano's, I didn't want him to pick me up because of what I had to do. I had to reveal my status after the fact. I was nervous and scared! Here we go again I thought to myself. Professor Maxwell walked in dressed in all black. He looked so sexy from head to toe. I couldn't believe I was in this situation, on a date with my Professor. What are the odds? I got up from my chair and received him with a genuine warm embrace. It was a dim lit setting. The restaurant that was filled with the smell of Italian food which was my favorite.

He sat down and looked into my eyes, we started off with small talk but I wanted to jump to the punch. "I have something to tell you Professor" I said. He had cut me off and began to seriously talk about dating. He talked about his goals in life, how beautiful I am to him and before I knew it the food was on the table and were were eating, laughing and drinking wine. Hours had past and the restaurant was basically empty. I knew I had to spit it out so that's exactly what I did.

"I have something to tell you, I need to get this out before we move any further", I said with a serious tone.

"Alright then Damien what is it?" said Professor Maxwell as he grabbed my hands and looked deep into my eyes.

I could tell he was concerned. I became very uncomfortable and slightly defensive with my demeanor because I have no idea how he would react to what I was about to tell him, so I quickly moved my hands.

"I'm HIV positive. I'm sorry, I know I should've told you before anything happened between us, if you never want to see me again I totally understand."

I thought to myself well that's not really possible, I have to see him in class, ugh this is crazy. I couldn't even look him in his eyes. My eyes became watery, not at the fact that I'm worried about his response but the fact that I even have to tell someone this. This is all still so new to me and I don't know if it will ever become easier.

Professor Maxwell's facial expression remained stern with a concerned look on his face. He didn't even flinch when the words came out. He stared at me for a moment and arose from his seat pulling his chair right next to me. He sat down and put his arm around me.

"You wouldn't be the first person I've dated with HIV. I respect your honesty and I definitely didn't make it easy for you to say no, but not everyone is going to be as understanding as me so you have to be careful Damien. I could have went off, this could've been a bad situation for you" said Professor Maxwell.

I shook my head agreeing with him, he spoke nothing but truth and I was better for it. I'm glad he didn't haul off and hit me but I know better now.

That night would be the first date of many. Everything always starts off so good and in our case it all seemed so perfect, we talked about everything. Professor Maxwell stayed guarded but, slowly but surely I would begin to break those walls down as he broke mine down "literally." We were having sex like crazy. I had so many new experiences with him, we took pictures together all the time.

It was almost like he was my secret and I wasn't going to kiss and tell about the way he did my body. He was so experienced and knew exactly where to touch me, where to taste me, and how to make me shake in pure ecstasy. It's like I wanted the whole world to experience the type of love he gave me. I had to tell somebody, and the only person I shared my secret love with was Lee. We had our arguments but we always made up and of course I was excelling in his class. I was falling for him, and I was falling fast. I felt like he wasn't going anywhere and neither was I.

I still talked to Christopher off and on and in between as the months past, I missed him but I was happy and he wasn't here with me. I deserved to be selfish and put myself first and that's exactly what I did.

Christopher knew it was someone else, and I believed he had found someone new as well. I made sure I didn't snoop, meaning I stayed my black ass off of his social media but from time to time I would find myself on his Instagram. I even found myself going through his likes and being petty. I hated the fact that I would do that but I was still in love with him. Many nights I cried out but he couldn't hear me, I cried words I never knew and in my heart I still held a light for him but he couldn't see it, so I let the light grow dim but never out.

Chapter Fourteen

"I Love You"

It was time for my 3 month checkup, I was so nervous, usually I'm talking all the time at every visit but this time was different. We were about to talk about my life, my health, my future. It's so crazy to me that everything is based on one small pill, "Don't miss a dose they say..." They have a pill, that can make me live a normal life span but they don't have a cure and its 2015. Hmmm makes me wonder about our society, our government. How can one little pill hold so much power but there's no cure.

I want to live and I'll do whatever I have to do in order to hold on just a little while longer. I know that no pill will determine my life span, only God can, I believe, I pray, and I truly want to live a long fulfilled life.

I won't stop fighting to live until it's my time to go and I know in the end, I will see his Glory. I believe that we all have our trials and tribulations in our lives and we should never give up. Giving up is never an option. I may have had that thought but we have so much to live for. I have so much to live for. So if you believe it, fight for it.

I want to get married, I want to have kids, I want to be normal and do what normal people do. The fact that Professor Maxwell is even going with me says a lot and it means a lot to me. I always wanted Christopher to be here but he never came.

Professor Maxwell and I walked into the doctor's office hand in hand.

"Hey love, Come on in Mr.Hill." said Nurse Jenny.

They were like a medical family to me of some sorts, oddly I have developed a good trusting relationship with them. "Damien, Lets check those vitals" said the nurse.

"Who is this man with you Damien" said the nurse with a big smile on her face.

Before I could open my mouth Professor Maxwell answered. "Well I'm his future husband, I'm Jose Maxwell." The nurse loved it and we both laughed, they always wanted to know about my dating life.

The Doctor walked in and smiled.

"Who is this" he said.

I responded and said "this is my other half, Jose."

The doctor looked at Jose, shook his hand and said "you better treat him right. He's a good one."

We proceeded to go over my vitals from 3 months ago, just to make sure everything is normal and I stayed undetectable. Which means it's extremely hard for me to pass the virus, like a 1 in a million chance. I could even have children and they wouldn't have the virus, technology is amazing. My CD4 count was over 1000 which means I'm very healthy and my viral load was undetectable. The doctor asked Jose if he had any questions.

"If I wanted to have unprotected sex with him, could I?" said Professor Maxwell.

"That's a good question" said the doctor, you can actually have unprotected sex with Damien if you wanted he said, but there are rules and guidelines to follow. There is now medication for someone who is not HIV positive to prevent the chance of contracting the virus. The medication is called Truvada. You both must be completely honest and monogamous because the medication does not prevent against other sexual transmitted diseases. It's safer for an HIV positive patient to be with a negative person because two positive people could actually make the virus worst. I know it's all very complicated but I recommend that you continue to practice safe sex unless you both are 100 percent sure you both are willing to take that step. I can definitely go into further detail and pull up statistics if you'd like."

Professor Maxwell looked at me and started smiling, he then winked.

"I've heard enough", I interjected. There will be no unprotected sex with me, I would feel absolutely horrible if I was the reason that someone had to go through such a life changing experience like me.

"So, get that thought out of your mind unless you're ready for marriage" I said playfully.

After we walked out of the doctor's office, I was very quiet, I was stuck in deep thought. The fact that I opened up to Professor Maxwell this much and shared with him such a serious part of my life is definitely a big deal.

"Ice cream" he said.

I laughed and said "you know it." We went to DQ and sat outside.

"So what's up Damien, how are you feeling?" Professor Maxwell asked.

"The question is how you are feeling Jose" I replied.

"Wow, did you actually say my name?" he laughed.

"I feel like I'm ready to go ring shopping" he said playfully.

"I'm serious" I said.

"I love you Damien Hill" said Professor Maxwell.

I was so shocked those words came out of his mouth. Those three words that mean so much to so many people. The words that have the power to change everything in one's world but not in mine, not anymore. Those three words don't mean anything to me. I've heard it all before and I was still left with a broken heart, not once but twice so I couldn't say the words back. That would be the wrong thing to do because I'll end up lying if I say I love you too. He knew it and I knew it. His demeanor changed when I didn't reiterate the words back.

"You don't have anything to say huh Damien."

"No I don't" I replied.

I wanted to tell him so bad that those words actually scare me now, those words don't mean shit to me.

"That's all I needed to hear" said Professor Maxwell.

Professor Maxwell grew cold and our time together grew short. He immediately said he had some paperwork to do. The ride home was quiet. No kiss or nothing as I got out of his car. I didn't want to think about it too much. Did I love him, am I falling in love with him. I honestly don't know. All I know is I'm happy with just him and I honestly don't want him to walk out of my life, like the rest.

Later that night, I was in my bed with my eyes closed and Christopher was all I could think of.

I closed my eyes and I began to cry. All the dark memories of Harris just came back flooding my mind. I remember when he first said I love you.

I was all in my feeling yet again, I was lonely and I missed Christopher. I missed his touch. All I needed was for him to hold me. When it's gets cold and I'm feeling kind of lonely he was always there to keep me warm. He was the cover that I needed and Professor Maxwell could never replace him.

"Please Christopher please come back" I said out loud as I cried myself to sleep.

Over the next couple of weeks Professor Maxwell would not talk to me outside of class. He was acting like a two faced little girl just like his zodiac sign. If you haven't guessed it. He was a Gemini and I'm a cancer. I tend to run off of pure emotion and I was fed up with the bullshit so on a break during my classes. I walked into his office and slammed the door.

"What the fuck is wrong with you" I said as I took a seat.

"I've been doing a lot of thinking and I love you Damien but I'm not in love with you" said Professor Maxwell.

"What the are you saying" I yelled.

"Please don't do this Damien, I was scared this might happen. Your still a baby and don't recognize a real man when he's in front of you. I refuse to waste your time or mine" said Professor Maxwell.

He looked me in my eyes and grabbed my hands.

"Do you understand what I mean" he said.

I'm so tired of playing these games with these men I thought to myself. I just don't get why everything has to be so complicated and the bullshit that just came out of his mouth was too much for me to even try to comprehend. I love you but I'm not in love with you. What the fuck does that mean? Have you ever heard such bull shit like that before? It's like I love you more than a friend but not enough to make it official. I looked Professor Maxwell in the face.

"I don't understand how you can say you love me but you're not in love with me. I don't understand how you can have sex with me and want to have unprotected sex with me and then want to stop dating me. I just don't" I replied

"I don't know what I want. I want you but I'm just not capable of giving you what you deserve. I can't give you 100 percent. I still have things that I'm dealing with and the more I get to know you the more I realize this isn't going to work. You deserve the world and I can't give that to you right now."

Its official I thought to myself, as smart as Professor Maxwell is, he's still a dumb confused ass Gemini and I'm not here for it.

I got up and I just walked away. I walked out the door and out of Professor Maxwell's live forever, even though I still have to see him in class. Truth be told I don't really know what I want but I know I don't want Professor Maxwell.

At this point I'm starting to believe that I'm going to be single forever. My heart has been broken so many times, and I continue to try and fix it on my own. I pray and say I trust God, but I never just be still and listen. I've tried to find love, without getting in touch with the real me. I just need change, and if being alone would bring forth that change, then so be it.

Chapter Fifteen

"Cherish These Moments of Life"

Weeks had went past and I was so glad that the semester was almost over. The break up or whatever you want to call it with Professor Maxwell, really wasn't that bad. For the first time in a long time, I was okay with just being alone. I've been reading my bible and staying focused on school and just catering to myself. I haven't thought about none of these men that act like little boys in forever. It's still odd when I attend class and Professor Maxwell walks in, but I'm focused. I know he still wants me but we will never be anything again. He's too old to be acting like a young boy trying to find his way, he should know what he wants by now. In his case he made the statistic true, that "men take a long time to mature."

I've been talking to Christopher a lot lately, almost every other day. We have been reading the bible together, I have been reading Psalms, the passage of prayers. We are both trying to apply God's word to our everyday lives. The long distance isn't even an issue anymore. I loved him and began to love his mother, somehow my heart still belongs to him. It feels so good to be back in church and to feel God's love meant all the world to me. In those times when I felt alone, I always keep in mind things could always be worse and I could make it. I have the lord and knowing he loves me keeps me warm at night, not a man.

My phone started to ring at 4:00 am Saturday morning, and it was Christopher's name that popped across my iPhone. I immediately answered.

"Baby" he said. I knew something was wrong from his tone.

"What's wrong Christopher?" He broke down crying, it was his mother I just knew it.

"What is it Christopher?"

"There saying she's not going to make it through the night Damien she's going to leave me."

"I'm so sorry baby, I'm so sorry" I replied, and tears started to fall from my eyes.

"I want to see you, I want to hold you, Can I please Face Time you?" Christopher said.

I popped my light on and I picked up his Face Time call. He was outside the hospital in his car, his eyes were blood shot red.

"Why would God take her from me Damien, tell me why?" Christopher yelled as the tears rolled.

At this point I don't know what to say, so I just let him vent. Nothing I could say right now would take away the pain that he felt concerning the health of his mother, but I knew she was strong and I believed she could make it through this.

"It's okay to cry baby let it out! I got you. I got your back but most of all the Lord has you, and she will make it through the night."

He finally looked up and looked into my eyes. I knew he really loved his mom, she was his heartbeat.

"You want to know what she told me last night, she said live your life baby and do what makes you happy."

"You know what Damien you make me happy. I've never stopped loving you and I'm coming home baby, I'm coming back to you if that's alright" Christopher said.

"Christopher now you know, that's alright. I love you" I said.

We sat and just talked and glared at each other for hours on Face Time. While he calmed down, I got comfortable on my bed. I needed to be there for him, like he has been there for me.

"Anything that you go through, I will always be there. We are in this together" I said. He started to cry again and so did I.

I began to pray out loud "Lord in you we trust, and in this moment of darkness, Lord we ask that you send your light. Show us your love Lord, Jesus please keep Loretta under your wings of healing. Please let her win this fight, let her see another day and add years to her life. Lord we come to you tonight asking for your blessings over her life. We are trusting in you and it is done. Amen!"

"Amen, thank you baby" Christopher said.

I can't imagine losing a parent so I stayed on Face Time with him until I fell asleep.

My phone began to ring at 8:00 am, it was Christopher, I'm hoping its good news.

"Hey baby, what's up" I said

"Baby she's alive and well. She is doing great, the Lord heard our prayers" Christopher said with excitement!

"That's great news and we have the Lord to thank for this. All we have to do is pray and believe" I replied.

"I meant everything I said last night, I'm coming back to you. Already talked it over with moms. It's Tuesday now, I'll be there Friday" Christopher said with even more excitement.

"I'll be waiting for you baby, I love you" I replied.

"I love you to peanut head" Christopher said before hanging up.

The rest of the week flew by and the semester was over. That means no more seeing Professor Maxwell's ass. No goodbye's, no let's be friends, no lets go to lunch, nothing. We were completely done and I was fine with that, besides its Friday and that means Christopher is on his way home to me. I received plenty of huge boxes from him throughout the week filled with his clothes and all of his miscellaneous stuff. He was such a man and I loved him, I spent the whole day talking off and on to Christopher making sure he was ok. I cleaned my little apartment until it was spotless, had to make sure it was able to fit me and Christopher's belongings. I was finally done cleaning, I cooked dinner and placed it on the table. I'm so excited, Christopher should be knocking at the door at any minute now.

I began to lay down on the couch, I was so exhausted. I laid flat on my back by the window I looked up at the ceiling then closed my eyes. I felt myself dosing off. I felt the warmth of the sun hit my face as the cool breeze caressed my skin. It made me smile, I was at peace and finally happy with my life.

I thought back to when I was depressed and couldn't climb out of my bitter state of being. We get so wrapped up with the idea of being in love, the idea of being in that fairy tale relationship. We get lost on the ride, on the journey the Lord has sat out for us.

It looks good on the outside but deep down we eventually learn that this person isn't the one for us, but instead of leaving we stay and fight for a relationship that isn't worth fighting for. So many times we ask ourselves why I still want you after all the things you've done to me. This is the very question I still can't answer. There are so many red flags and signs that are thrown in our face and yet we are lost in this false reality ignoring every warning.

You know what I think, I think that every relationship is a learning experience. Each day that goes by we grow smarter, wiser, and stronger. It's time for me to let go of my hate, and let go of my past! I am not normal, I am a unique and special individual. Every day that goes by I realize I live a blessed life, and God loves me and I can feel his love. I've been on this ride since day one and I'm finally letting my inhibitions go.

No more hatred or resentment will be held in my heart towards anyone. I've allowed these men to drive me all over the place physically, mentally, and spiritually. Sometimes in life we lose our way, and allow situations or people to be our driving force. I allowed Harris, Christopher and, Professor Maxwell to be the driver and that ends today. There is only one driver, and his name is Jesus Christ the savior of the world. God has always been in control, and I'm enjoying this ride. Learning to trust him more than I ever did before. Life is what you make it, and we must all go through some sort of storm but just know you're not alone. You are never alone, he hears your cries, he listens and gives us the answers and I've received my answer. I'm going to live and be prosperous.

Suddenly there's a knock on the door. I arose with excitement because it could only be one person at the door, and that's Christopher. I looked out the window and the sun was setting, and he's just now getting here. Must've been bad traffic, but I don't care my Prince Charming was at my door and baby I am the prize. I jumped off the couch, gave myself a quick mirror check, mouth washed and ran to the door. I swung that bad boy open and to my dismay Professor Maxwell was at my door.

"Awww shit" I said out loud.

"Good to see your sarcasm hasn't went anywhere" Professor Maxwell said as he walked in the door.

"We need to talk Damien, I miss you" said Professor Maxwell.

"I can't do this right now Professor, can we please talk later?" I replied

Our conversation was interrupted by more knocks at my door. This time harder and with more force.

Oh my God, I thought to myself that's Christopher.

"You gotta go, that's my man at the door" I said

"Your man" Professor Maxwell said in confusion.

"Yes, my man, the one I'm in love with" I said.

Excitement took over me once again, I ran to the door with every intention of jumping into his arms, wrapping my legs around him and kissing him down.

I swung the door open and froze in my tracks.

"Hello, Are you Damien Hill?" said the male police officer.

"Yes, I am officer" I said with a concerned tone. Professor Maxwell walked up to the door.

"There's been an accident" said the female police officer.

"What kind of accident" asked Professor Maxwell

"Do you know Christopher Brown" said the male officer.

"Yes, Yes I do, what happened, is he okay" I said while trying not to panic.

"He was ran off the road while heading to this location, he landed in a ditch totaling his car" said the female police officer.

"Is he alive" I yelled out.

They both looked at each other.

"What do you mean, RAN off the road, IS HE ALVIE?" I yelled out at both of them.

Professor Maxwell quickly put his arms around me to calm me down. I needed answers and I needed them now.

"We need you to go down to the station with us" said the female police officer.

"To the station, for what? "said Professor Maxwell

"Is He alive?" I yelled out as the tears started to flow.

"I'm sorry young man but Christopher Brown died upon impact and you were the last person he contacted" said the female police officer.

"NO, no, nooo" I screamed out in pain. How could this happen, How could this be, I thought to myself. Professor Maxwell still held me to console me, I knew I had to be having a crazy day dream again. This couldn't be reality, he couldn't be dead. I just spoke with him not too long ago.

Everything started to move in slow motion and my breathing became sporadic. I dropped to the floor and began to count, in an attempt to calm myself. I started rocking, counting from 10 to 1, so that when I hit one I could awake from this nightmare. 10,9,8.....3,2,1 I opened my eyes and I was still on the floor. Everyone tried to get me up, I just couldn't move.

I went back in my mind, to my memories with Christopher to try and pull back every good memory we had to drown out this darkness that overcame me. I thought about him coming over to study with me, and cooking my favorite meals. I even thought about him waiting patiently for me to be honest about my status, and not judge me in any way. Then it hit me hard that this might just be real life. My Prince Charming is gone. My baby isn't coming through that door to rescue me. I screamed and I yelled. It felt like a piece of my heart, the piece that had just been healed was being ripped out from my chest. Christopher Brown is DEAD. My one true love. The one thing that I tried to hold on too.

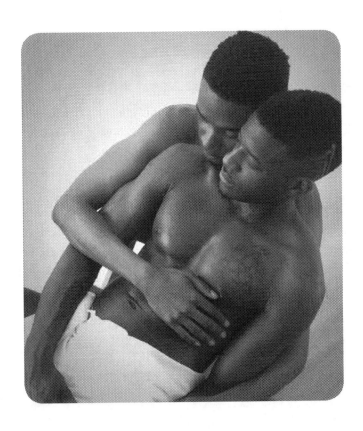

About the Author

Matthew Tayvonne is a young, elite, up-and-coming author and a college graduate with a master's degree in counseling. His home town is Cleveland, Ohio, but he is now residing in Atlanta, Georgia, where he continues his journey to the top as an author. He is also now CEO of the website, TheUtopiaSuite.com—a site for erotic stories and commentary on the entertainment world.

Tayvonne's drive and ambition is an unstoppable force fueled by Jesus Christ and the love of his family and close friends. But his writing is more than erotic and explicit stories. There is a meaning behind each story, and within this three-part book series, you may come to understand life is a gift and we must live it to the fullest.

Printed in the United States
By Bookmasters